SHADOWS AND ILLUSIONS

Francisco Gross

Contents

°111°

- -

THEY SAY GOOD things take time and I believe I am a good thing, the best even, and that's why I'm always late.

At least that's the excuse I tell myself time and time again. It's the one thing that's echoing repeatedly in my head as Reagan pulls up her car in front of my office building.

Scrambling around the car, I gather my littered files from the floor and groan. My black chiffon top sticks to my back like a scared child holding on to his parent in a horror house despite the frosty February morning.

The ripping of paper resounds and I swear beneath my breath. That had better not be anything about the presentation I'm about to give.

My best friend and roommate, Reagan chuckles by my side. The sound fills the car with warmth and a teasing taunt. "Would you take it easy, Lee? I keep telling you we have the technology to make things easier for you and yet you keep carrying your stack of papers around."

I pause my scrambling and raise my head to send her a menacing look.

Her sienna brown close-set eyes twinkle with mischief not fazed by my glare that keeps people away from me most of the time and she laughs with her long, black hair fixed in a ponytail, bobbing around.

"I love my papers and they love me too. See?" I raise a sheet that mocks me with its rumpled state. Rolling my eyes, I drop the paper straightening the edges, and look back at Reagan who has a raised eyebrow amused at my situation. "Besides, if you wanted me to have a peaceful morning, why didn't you hurry me up? I woke up earlier than normal, for goodness' sake!" I whine.

"Yes, you did," she replies, her rosebud lips curled up with a teasing smile. "But you took more time to get ready than you normally do, too. Thought you had a lot of time on your hands, you said."

"Oh, shut up."

Yes, I definitely did. I took my precious time once again to get ready. But I won't blame myself because my brain is just wired that way. I see the extra time and I take things slowly because I'm a good thing. Remember?

"Haveal would literally kill me this time," I mutter, stumbling out of the car with my mess.

"Oh, don't be so dramatic. The young boss is so small and fragile, he couldn't even hurt a fly if he wanted to."

Laughter escapes my lips before I can help it. "Oh honey," I say, shaking my head at her naivety. "His stature says absolutely nothing about him. The man can summon the fiery pits of hell to the earth and not get burned. Got to go!"

Ice crackles beneath my feet as I sprint towards the freakish tall skyscraper that stretches towards heaven, presuming that soaking up the goodness would make the glass building any less daunting. On its front, the name of the company is engraved with a font as formidable as the building itself 'Shaveal Robotics Limited'.

"Break a leg at your presentation, literally!" Regan shouts, and I send her a view of my exceptional middle finger just before I get into the building, not bothering to look back at her.

The hair on my neck raises once I step into the building courtesy of the horrid stares people send my way. I spare them no glance as I hurry further to the receptionist's desk.

I know how I might look right now, but why should that bother me when I have my sweet haven? The one that will make everything alright. Having your office on the 75th floor comes with its perks. You have just enough time to gather yourself together within the elevator as it goes all the way up.

Little miniature robots whiz by me in my journey forward, almost making me lose my steps. Thank goodness for quick reflexes. I flick a gaze at them for a moment with a smile. Oh, such promises, these little ones show.

"You look like you're late again," A chirpy voice says to me from behind the desk.

I turn to the young receptionist and give her my signature grin. She's busy moving things around her desk tidying up the already clean place, her shoulder-length silver-grey hair popping against her tawny-colored skin, flips to the side with eyes matching her hair, giving me an incredulous gaze.

"Mia honey, who is Kalisha Morales without being late?"

The ticking of the clock just behind her gains my attention and deters me from the scowl that adorns her face.

Well, shoot! I'm 20 freaking minutes late!

I send Mia a soft smile, gather my scattered belongings and run ahead to the elevator. The door to the elevator closes as I get near it.

"Hold it, please!" I screech, stretching my hands forward and adding more momentum to my feet. Not that I was ever an athlete, to begin with...

A peach-colored calloused hand stretches out of the elevator just before I get there. "Thank you!" A relieved breath breaks out of my lips as I dive straight into the elevator.

Once the door closes behind me and the elevator jerks, rising, I throw my head backward, taking deep breaths in. After getting my racing heart under control, I move to the metallic keypad by the door, ready to type in my floor number.

Since there are a lot of floors, Haveal figured having a series of buttons lines up there would be too oppressing, so everyone gets to type in the floor they're going to on the metallic keypad.

75

It reads by the side, already typed in. Oh, a colleague? I turn to my side to look and the fellow companion of my elevator and floor and I can't help but whistle once I set my eyes on him.

He becomes even stiffer as I press my lips against each other.

Oops, I really need to pull myself together but damn, do people like this exist in the real world?

With his jet black hair in a sleek style adorning his perfectly sculptured face and a few days' growths of beard on his chiseled jaw, the man can be described as nothing else but being hot like fire.

Woohoo! He's definitely no colleague of mine, but the name tag on his shirt gives away his identity: Andres Anderson.

A smirk appears on his full cupid's bow lips at my unabashed staring and my lips lift into a grin, fixing my posture and ready to get my flirt on but his tall and muscular body remains in its fixed position, making no move to turn in my direction.

Are we playing hard to get Mr. Handsome Andres?

Or is it courtesy of the way I look? My monstrous reflection across from me glares at me. Well, that can't benefit me.

I turn to the panel above the keypad.

Floor 30.

It's time to fix things. Let's see how you play hard to get once I'm done, stranger. I'm a work of art myself once cleaned up if I should say so myself.

Turning to the side, I drop my bag and files beside me on the floor. My glacial blue eyes stare back at me and I can't help but wink. One of the many outstanding features I inherited from my mother.

That's including my curly midnight black voluminous hair that I tie up to look presentable to make my diamond-shaped face pop and excluding my 5'6 height.

After puckering my lush thin lips to add lipstick there, my eyes flicker to Andres, my perfect stranger, and I see his sharp icy blue eyes already set on me.

Already checking me out, I see.

I gracefully pick my stuff up from the floor. Unfortunately, my top allows no cleavage to show. That would have added to the charm, but I give him a flirtatious smile.

Reagan says my smile can make men fall into the scurry pits of hell with no complaints. Let's see how true that is. Not that I want him to go to hell or anything like that.

I expect a flirtatious remark or a snarky one at the very least, but all I get is nothing but the creaking of the elevator going up.

Floor 65.

Turning rigidly back to the front, I wonder just how difficult it is to flirt with someone.

The ever spacious, which is always a comfort, as it prevented unnecessarily grazing of bodies against each other, suddenly feels too big. Its size gives me no excuse to stumble into him by accident.

Floor 68.

How does one stand beside such a gorgeous human being and not say something, anything at all? It's depressing.

The elevator quakes faintly and I hold on to the railing by my side promptly with wide eyes.

Floor 69

Floor 70

It slammed to a halt so fast my light grip on the railing does nothing to prevent me from crashing forward against the elevator walls. I moan at the impact of the metal against my skin.

Before I can fully grasp what is going on, the lights flicker off, letting the darkness consume the entire elevator.

What? Really? You want to do this right now?!

My breaths come in short and fast as I try to calm myself down.

It's all right. The emergency light would turn on. Everything would be just fine but it doesn't become fine because that doesn't happen.

Damn you, Treyvon. How difficult is it to do just the job of keeping the elevator working at all times?

I need to get out if I still want to have my job by the end of the day, for goodness sake.

Blinking a few times helps my eyes adjust a bit to the darkroom and I snatch my bag up from my feet, rummaging through it for my phone.

My hand grazes over keys, documents, everything but the phone itself, and I groan, already feeling overheated. At long last, I locate the phone and a shaky breath breaks out. "Thank goodness," I mutter.

That's when it occurs to me that there's been no remark from my handsome stranger. Is he still trying to act all tough?

Turning on the flashlight on my phone, I raise it up to search for Andres and a foreign high-pitched shriek escapes my lips. My phone slips immediately from my hand, falling to the ground with a crack as I flinch backward against the walls of the elevator with my heart pounding like never before.

Time seems to slow down as I stare directly into the icy blue eyes of Andres, that has now become cold and lifeless looking.

He opens his mouth to speak and a deep baritone voice that would have sent any woman in a normal circumstance melting merges from his lips, sending discomforting tingles through my skin.

"You have no idea who I am, do you?"

▫ · ☐☐☐☐☐☐ · ₪ · ☐☐☐☐☐☐ · ▫

✎ WORD COUNT: 1840

Vote, Comment, and Share if you enjoyed it!

Beautiful cover above by:

▫ · ☐☐☐☐☐☐ · ₪ · ☐☐☐☐☐☐ · ▫

°121°

□ · □□□□□□ · ₪ · □□□□□□ · □

AS THE TINGLING in my skin drags on, my stomach clenches. Staring into his cold dead eyes feels awfully close to being forced down into a tank filled with icy lake water and not allowed to resurface.

Every part of my being feels like it's drowning as my thoughts scramble about, trying to get a grasp on the whole situation.

Who he is? Who is he?

In the heat of the moment, I try desperately to remember this man. Working my brain on overdrive trying to think and reflect, but my memories pull up with no recognition of a man named Andres Anderson. There is no trace. It's a blank slate.

His head tilts slightly to the side and with it, his lips curl up into a sinister smile that pushes me further into the freezing cold water I've found myself in. He moves so slowly and precisely, I almost think I'm imagining it till a silver shining object reflects in his eyes.

A KNIFE?

I hurriedly try to back away from him. My heart hammers in my chest as I stagger backward, putting as much space as I can between us.

Is this a joke? What sort of silly prank is this?

"A- a- andres?" I stutter, my regularly warm voice sounding so foreign in my ears. "Y- you're Andres, right? We can talk about it, I promise, t- there's really no need for violence." My back hits the chilly metal wall of the elevator and I shiver, but I don't stop moving and instead change direction, not even sure if he's following me or not. "L- listen, I'm not that difficult, really? You can just give me a hint of where we know each other from and I'll remember. Honestly..."

"She talks too much! She talks TOO MUCH!" Andres yells, his voice rattling the entire elevator as it echoes back and forth, sending cold shivers rushing through my entire body, leaving goosebumps in its wake.

His speech is all the warning I get before he swings the hand holding the knife in my exact direction.

I collapse at the very last minute, stumbling over myself just before the knife can graze my skin. Turning back to him with even wider eyes, my brain slowly tries to grasp how dire this whole mess may be.

"Stop running," he slurs. "It makes me mad. You don't want to see me mad."

Yeah right. Put the knife down and maybe I'll consider that.

My mind is in disarray. Everything seems like a blur and the direction of things appears to have vaporized from my mind with my sole focus being nothing but trying to get as far from him as humanly possible. This will also mean getting out of this elevator; I just need to find the keypad.

Where is it?

"Kali."

My entire body freezes down to my erratic beating heart, and my mouth immediately becomes drier than the Sahara.

How? How did he... No one. No one calls me Kali except him.

"Don't run from me, Kali."

His voice resonates louder, showing that he's closer but that's the least thing grabbing my attention, and this takes with it the will of my body to move. Nothing seems to work, no matter how hard I try.

Him?

No.

That's not right, he can't be here.

A lump forms in my throat as lights in my head rapidly, hoping desperately that it's not him.

It's just a coincidence, Lee. It's nothing but that. Your name is Kalisha. Of course, someone would call you Kali. It is the most obvious nickname, right?

"Gotcha!"

His voice booms right by my ear, filled with too much excitement, and a shrill escapes my lips just as a static noise erupts from behind us, stopping all movements.

"Hi! Is anyone there? This is Treyvon Ward..."

My lips part as a burst of light shaky laughter escapes from it. I quickly use the opportunity of his divided attention to scramble away from Andres.

Right, what was I thinking? Him? Here? It's not possible, he can't be here.

"We're working on getting the lights back on. Please stay calm..."

The lights flicker back on instantly and I shut my eyes close immediately at the sudden change in the room, but my breathing slows down as I calmly open my eyes again.

The feeling of relief doesn't last long as I realize Andres moved at the same time I did. He's there by the keypad and...

Suddenly it feels like there's no air in my lungs anymore.

Is- is that the knife he was holding before?

The light tones down its shine but I miscalculated . That is no small kitchen knife, it's a freakishly big one that looks ready to follow the instructions of its master to cut off the life of its prey.

He turns to me with a smirk and a glint that solidifies the plan he has in mind. I shake my head rapidly. No!

"N..." I open my mouth to say, but he's already brought down his hand to the keypad just as Treyvon's voice makes another announcement.

Locating me with ease, thanks to the now lit place and with no time for delay, Andres pushes forward, charging straight at me. I try to move, I honestly do, but it happens with a certain speed I will never expect someone of his build to ever manage or execute.

Just as he raises his hand with the knife to have a go at me, the lights in the elevator flicker back off and the room quivers suddenly, propelling him forward with even more momentum than before and sends me backward with my back hitting the cool wall with unwarranted force.

My breath gets stuck in my throat at the pain that erupts through my body. Even with that, I freeze up awaiting the pain from the knife contacting my body but I feel nothing. All I hear is the clanging of his knife against the elevator wall right by my side.

Did he miss? But how?

A sudden frustrating growl resounds through the elevator, causing my body to shudder and retreat.

"Where are you?!"

My gaze darts around the elevator since my eyes have adjusted to the darkness by now. I try to get a grasp on what's going on at the moment.

He's looking around the place everywhere but in my direction, right by his side.

Just how did he miss?

He got me the first time. If he can't see in the dark, how did he...?

I scoff internally as realization sets in. I was talking, rambling on, and trying to reason with him. Of course. If he can't see in the dark, he would use any sound I make to locate me. This also means what he lacks with his eyes, he makes up for it with a precise accuracy with his ears.

"Kali!" His voice booms a lot thicker and harsher than before, expressing the limit of his patience.

But then, why... why would he make the lights go off?

He didn't know.

It is the only plausible explanation.

He doesn't know because he doesn't work here. If he does, he will know the light going off after destroying the keypad is a safety measure I put in place just for the fun of it. Haveal has never seen a proposal on it or even approved one as it is a recent experiment but one known by every other employee.

If he didn't know the lights would go off since it had come on, he will think to destroy my contact with the outside world while still trapping me and dealing with me with ease.

"KALI!"

The clashing of his knife against the elevator walls reverberates through the room with him moving around slashing in any direction, hoping to hear a whimper when the knife touches me.

My breaths, short, go in quick successions as everything settles within my mind. There's a light leap in my heart at this conclusion. There might as well be hope for me. All I have to do is move around, making no sound that could draw him to me.

That shouldn't be too hard, right? Just have to be as silent as a graveyard.

But even as this swift feeling of relief fills me, I can't help but wonder. Who is Andres Anderson, and what could he possibly want with me?

□ · □□□□□□ · ₪ · □□□□□□ · □

✎Word Count: 1406

✎Total Word Count: 3246

Vote, Comment, and Share if you enjoyed it!

□ · □□□□□□ · ₪ · □□□□□□ · □

°131°

□ · □□□□□□ · ₪ · □□□□□□ · □

THE LIGHT IS an easy feat to maneuver, but the dark is an entirely distinct case. It sucks in all the different shades of colors that fill one's eyes in the light replacing it with gray monotones. The advantage of moving in the mass of the gray monotones needs a skill, one that it seems Andres lacks, and to be completely honest, so do I.

Everything can go wrong right here in the darkness, but I take in a deep breath, trying to calm my heart rate that seems to want to spike out of proportion. That proves very difficult with the tightness forming in my chest because there's only one thing that can make things go my way here, and it is if I can move around and see through the darkness without making any sound.

I close my eyes and apply pressure to it with my hands. Studious Reagan says it helps the eyes adjust to the darkness. I open them immediately, locking my gaze toward the last clang against the wall, determined for things to go my way.

It all seems blurry, but I can make out the foggy shapes of black and white from the reflection of a few things around the elevator, forcing a soft breath out of my lips. But I don't dwell on this because if I'm right, then the biggest gray monotone would be Andres and he's heading straight for me.

I swiftly move away from his direction. My heart struggles against my ribcage, ready to burst out as I remove my heels, not leaving anything to chance. The clang of his knife against the aluminum walls right just where I am crams the elevator and vibrates through the walls, disclosing his frustration.

Well, looks like we're getting to each other, buddy!

"Till when?!" he exclaims. His voice bounces off the walls. "Till when are we going to play this game of hide and seek, Kali? You can delay it for as long as you want, but your sweet blood will drip down my knife sooner or later."

The strength and confidence of his voice make me gulp hard at the hidden promise in that statement. His lack of sight is a weakness, but one he draws a veil over with his confidence. This literally drags my effort to use his weakness against him in the mud.

No. Jokes on you, buddy. I won't let your knife touch my blood. Definitely not that.

I need to get out of here!

Do you need help to get out of a stuck elevator? Pull me.

The words suddenly flash within my mind and I whip my head subconsciously in the direction where Andres is standing. I am not focused on him directly but on what should be right behind him.

Crap.

You know that moment when you need a piece of information that you should know but you didn't know you knew, but when you need it; it comes to you?

No? Oh well, this is that moment for me.

When the lights came on earlier, there was just that brief second to take in my surroundings and I noticed that flashy yellow sign with those words. It meant nothing to me before, but if I really want out of here, I have to take my chances.

Sure, trusting a sign like that in this elevator seems like nothing but reaching and having false hope, but that's all I can do. Grab onto thin threads that can be nothing but an illusion.

I focus on the task at hand. If I have to do anything, I have to do it now.

I need him to move away from where he is.

But how do I freaking get him to go far away without him suspecting me?

Think! Think, Lee, Think! You're an engineer, a smart one. You should know how to maneuver your way around here.

My body vibrates with desperation, trying to figure out an escape route by playing out scenarios at which this can go. My fingers twitch around the shoes I currently have in my hands and the chill of the elevator suddenly becomes hot as my eyes tighten, examining the elevator space around me and hoping the shadows of the dark can be my guide.

I choke at the sudden movement by my side and my thoughts come to a sudden halt, realizing that my split second of distraction has gotten him close to me.

This forces me to move instantly with my current rigid posture. I grunt as a jab of pain shoots through me when my wrist comes in contact with the wall by the side from landing in an improper position.

Shoot! Not now, you idiot! You shouldn't make a sound.

Needing to get him far away from where I need to go and from me, I waste no time checking if he heard my hiss. My arm which, thankfully I didn't sprain, grips the shoe in it harder and I hurl the heel straight away from me. The crack against the wall resonates through gaining Andres' attention.

The husky sound of his laughter bounces off in excitement.

"Couldn't keep still anymore, Kali?" he asks and dashes forward in that direction.

It worked?

Doesn't matter. Move! Now!

The want to ease up in relief at being able to fool him surges through me but I shut it down instantly and instead I move my feet to where I need them to go. I finally feel grateful for the large space within this elevator unlike earlier on.

No matter what happens, he won't get to me quick enough.

With every hit of my feet against the floor, the soothing cold surges up my feet and clashes with the warmth of my blood produced by my erratic, beating heart. Goosebumps lay on its wake atop my skin and

I almost want the comfort of my heels back, but it's a luxury I can't afford.

Instead, I move with the precision and calculation of a chess player who knows a single blunder could ruin the entire game. That is a step I can't make.

But with my focus being just on reaching my destination, I pay less attention to the distracted Andres.

And in that lies my undoing.

The swoosh of the little air right behind me bringing the promise of force slams the object it carried straight into me. I miss a step and stumble backward into the wall behind me.

Hot agony slices through my nerves down to my bones and a shrill escape from my lips captures the space of the elevator. The pounding in the back of my head replaces any sensible thoughts that can go on within my head.

With the agony growing in me, my hand graces over the item that hit me and in that moment, I know I am done for.

My shoe.

So, there was a blunder, after all.

How- how did he- But he can't see in the dark, right?

"Thought you could fool me?!"

Everything seems like a blur of movement, but I can make out his silhouette charging right back. The sound from the impact, my scream, and whatever other information that I'm missing tells me he's coming in my precise direction.

My heart pounds even faster to an unbelievable pace as I wearingly lay down my options. It is either I change my direction to confirm if he can see in the dark or reach out to pull the one thing that seems to be my only hope.

"Watch me make your blood mine."

"No!" I grit out with forced restraint.

I can't give up now. I push forward despite the closeness he has on me. If the card is the real deal, a solution was there right at my fingertips. And if it works, then I won't have to deal with the repercussions of Andres' knife, but if not, there might be no fooling him anymore.

No matter what I'm getting out of this inconvenience right this minute.

My hands reach for the wall close to the paper, searching for the handle or whatever I'm meant to pull. My breaths go in short and fast and the hairs on my back tell of the ever-growing presence behind me, but I don't stop until my hand graces a handle.

At that moment, it feels like time slows down.

My grip tightens on the handle and his presence strengthens and becomes ever more present right behind me.

This is deciding moment. It's now or never.

I pull on the handle with all my strength and my breath hitches in anticipation.

□ · □□□□□□ · ₪ · □□□□□□ · □

✎Word Count: 1442

✎Total Word Count: 4688

Vote, Comment, and Share if you enjoyed it!

□ · □□□□□□ · ₪ · □□□□□□ · □

°141°

☐ · ☐☐☐☐☐☐ · ₪ · ☐☐☐☐☐☐ · ☐

LIFE PRIDES ITSELF in packing the unexpected into freaking large baggage and crushing whosoever it wants with it.

It turns out I'm the next unsuspecting victim.

A peal of ear-splitting laughter bursts out of the speakers in the elevator immediately I pull the handle. I freeze, with my muscles tightening up from the ringing in my ears as a knot voluntarily tenses beyond comfort in my stomach. Nausea hits in a shocking wave.

My brows furrow and my eyes search around me with just one question stuck in my head.

What. The. Hell. Just. Happened?

As if sensing the question in my head, Andres, who has stopped moving at the sound of the laughter, fills the elevator with the sound of his own laughter. "You thought you could escape?"

The husky sound pulls on the strings of anger growing within by the minute. Every bit of shock wears off as my fists tighten, probably turning my knuckles white.

"It must suck, huh? After trying all your possible best to distract me and all of that was for naught? I am quite disappointed though, Kali, that you fell for that trick. Is this how useless you are now?"

Useless.

I am up on my feet before I know it, ignoring the loud screaming in my head telling me to back down. There's no plan because when has there ever been one? But I don't care because all I know is I'm done. I'm done taking bashes from a guy who should know absolutely nothing about me.

Just who does he think he is?

Grabbing hold of the shoe previously thrown back at me, I launch an attack on him.

Everything is wrong with this action of mine from the fact that he's got a whole one foot over me and a lot of pounds, along with the point that he's the one holding the real weapon. But with the way my muscles quiver and heat rushes through my body, all these things seem to be nothing but a little discomfort.

I cannot keep going around in this mess. If I want out, it's about time I face Andres head-on.

Plugging into the steaming anger coursing through my veins, I charge forward, colliding straight into Andres, knocking him off balance. His shoes screech against the floor in response. Taking advantage of his discord, I waste no time swinging a kick at his hands holding the knife.

The clang of the knife falling onto the floor resounds through the room.

I groan internally.

That is definitely not where I wanted the knife to end up. I needed it closer to me to turn the tides around in my favor.

Andres stumbles forward at the kick and with him being by my side, I send my elbow backward into his unprotected side. Pain tears through my elbow at the contact and water pools in my eyes, but I push aside my emotions.

Now is not the time to think or feel anything. All I need to do is focus.

Andres sneers at me. "You want to play dirty, huh?"

A fierce throb explodes in my side from a punch he lands there. The sensation ripples in three folds once he latches onto my hands and flips me over. I land with a hard thump on the floor, gasping for air.

I tighten my fists through the pain. Bastard. I grab onto his leg that's right by my side and pull hard, ignoring the burning protest of my muscles at the action.

He drops to the floor with a resounding clang and I push myself up, ready to take charge of the situation once again.

"You've been playing dirty all day. Now it's my time."

Pure rage crosses my face as I lurch forward. He's up on his feet almost immediately, and he maneuvers away from my attack, but I don't allow him any further than that.

There's no time for that!

Keep going even if they seem big. Just keep striking till you find a weakness you can exploit and you hit that hard.

My mother's words ring in my head loud and clear, powering me up with all I need to keep going. The beads of sweat trickling down my back do nothing to sway my determination. I keep going, hitting him while he counters, but I'm winning. Groans fill up the air, one after another, till a final grunt from Andres pushes him to the floor with me standing.

This is it. This is my moment.

You're not taking me down, Andres. I am.

Advancing forward, my feet hit something strong like iron and my heart leaps up in pure joy.

Of course, there will be something to strike him with, especially since he went around brandishing his knife. It's time to finish up what you started Andres.

Just a little more, Lee, and you'll be fine.

I pick up the rod from the floor with my fists that's all right, but I freeze on the spot as soft, mocking laughter reaches my ears.

I scoff inwardly. Nothing can get me to back down now, not even his weak attempt at disarming me.

It will not work!

My body feels heavy with every step I take, but I can't stop now. Not at this point where I'm so close to victory.

But the victory is only my fantasy.

The sound of his laughter increases as he rises from the door. There's no grunt of pain or anything that can make me think he was in a fight he was losing.

He turns to me fully, standing straight right in front of me with a smile that wiped away the existence of everything that had just happened.

The rod falls from my hands. The clang of its hit against the floor matches the shocking waves flooding my body at the moment.

Andres leaves no time for me to take in what's going on. He throws a punch straight for my stomach and another rage of pain erupts through me, straight down to my bones. A pained grunt escapes my lips, stumbling backward straight into the wall behind me. I bend over, coughing repeatedly.

He shouldn't- He shouldn't be this strong, not after...

The laughter continues pouring from his lips and it backs up my strength straight down inside of me. I stand straight, groaning as I put pressure on my injured wrist, but I just crumble back against the wall.

What is going on?

I can't... I can't seem to keep going. It's like the turn of events has left me high and dry with nothing but the question of how, left.

How did this happen? How did it all go wrong?

"You must have thought you were winning, didn't you?"

A fist connects to my unprotected jaw next, and my head whips backward. An intense pain explodes in my head at the impact that feels like multiple double-edged swords being driven into every inch of my body.

My vision gets cloudy and the shades of grey that filled it with a certain amount of comfort previously are suddenly becoming darker.

He tsks his lips as I stumble to the floor, unable to hold myself up again. "Oh, poor you. You used all that strength and you never even hit me fully once."

I choke and my eyes open wide like saucers.

What is he talking about?

"That's not- that's not possible, I.."

His continuous laughter drowns out my remaining words, but even if it didn't, no words can flow out of my mouth. Every little warning from earlier on fills my head on repeat.

You didn't. You didn't hit him.

"You did nothing, sweet Kali. Nothing at all."

Useless.

I shake my head vigorously with the little strength I have with my insides tearing to pieces.

I can't let him do this to me. No, I won't let him. I'm not useless, I'm...

But you did nothing at all.

"That was so much fun." He crouches before me instantly and I move backward on instinct, but it only causes the pang in my head to increase once my head hits the wall, as there is no more space between the wall and myself.

The smirk on his face flashes before my eyes right before he grabs hold of my chin, forcing it up to look him in the eye with a strength that rivals what any human should have at this point that we have reached.

"You must have thought you were living up to your name once more, huh? Kalisha, lucky. But you've got no luck, Kalisha, not anymore."

The words crash down on my already weakened body, forcing me to swallow hard. Any fight that will have been able to find a retort dies down with the crash. There is no struggle left anymore, after all, if it isn't the truth and the luck in my name that has pushed me through life every day, the one luck that made me confident to take my time and believe that I'm good, is still available, I wouldn't be down here at the mercy of this stranger.

"Well, now, it's my turn to live up to my name."

Time stills at his declaration, taking its time to move, and it almost seems like thrusting his confident smirk is all it takes to live up to his name.

But no matter how long it feels like it happened, it is all but a moment and then it all finally makes sense.

Hot agony slices through my body as the knife I didn't notice him pick up pierces through me and my blood oozes out from the point of contact.

There's no air.

It...

My breaths go in quick and shallow, but no oxygen seems to want to flow into my body.

Time suddenly feels like it is tired of moving. It was running out.

My trembling hands move, wanting to put a stop to the pain, but his hand over the knife tightens and I suck in a sharp breath at the pain soaring through him. He bends down ever so slightly, placing his mouth next to my ear.

"At the end of the day, your sweet blood got on my knife."

□ · □□□□□□ · ₪ · □□□□□□ · □

✎Word Count: 1709

✎Total Word Count: 6397

Vote, Comment, and Share if you enjoyed it!

□ · □□□□□□ · ₪ · □□□□□□ · □

°151°

□ · □□□□□□ · ₪ · □□□□□□ · □

THE PAIN YOU feel today would be the strength you feel tomorrow, they say. Whoever came up with that has definitely not had pain explode in them, ripping through every inch of their body like it's doing in mine.

It consumes all of my senses and I lose track of where I am. Laughter flashes in and out of my head, but nothing is consistent.

The pressure is suddenly gone and my hands resume their previous mission. With the knife gone, the blood flows right out of its regular home into a cold, hard world.

My hands grace the sticky liquid, and I choke back a breath.

Blood. My blood.

My head becomes like it is an enormous weight on my body. It's heavy and beginning to slip off.

I know it's futile and it most certainly won't do me any good, but like before, I can't help it as my hands leave the gushing wound to my eyes' point of view.

It's still dark and I can't see the blood. My hands have also become nothing but a blurry mist. The pressure of the stickiness on my hand is all my brain needs to generate an image so vivid, the air around me feels too constricted.

Time becomes just another insignificant factor as the real darkness begins to cloud my vision. Every part of me turns tense from a sudden realization.

This is it. This is where I die. After everything I did, this is where it all ends.

The tears pour down my ears like a large fountain placed in the world to see. My heart wrenches into a million pieces in tow.

How did it all come down to this?

It's the last thing I think of before my body goes numb and I let the darkness take over.

I can't fight anymore. I give up.

"That's it?! You're just going to give up like that?!" A familiar yet distant cold and deep voice snaps at me.

This causes my heart to pick up a pace in contrast to its previous stagnant one.

"Just a little bleeding is what it takes for you to give up?"

As he keeps talking, the voice becomes much clearer, but I can't see him. Everything is still dark. I can't feel anything. Am I standing? Am I sitting? The hairs on my back stand tall but I can't feel my body.

What on earth is going on here? Where am I? Am I dead?

"Not yet. But you will be if you don't get up and do something about it!"

"Theo? Theodore? What are you doing here?"

His auburn, sleek hair is the first thing that makes it out of the darkness before the rest of his face joins in.

I choke back my tears in relief.

The familiarity of his chiseled, sculptured face that I loved to stare at just for the fun of it warms me up for a moment. But the lush lips that were always set into a thin line and chestnut eyes that told everyone who came across them to beat it in the office, are now downcast with strong disappointment written all over them.

He's here.

How is he here?

"Are you just going to let him finish you up because your luck ran out? Is that it?"

"But there's nothing. There's really nothing I can do, Theodore. I'm bleeding out and weak and useless."

He scoffs, shaking his head. "Who knew the great Kalisha was nothing but a quitter?"

"What? You don't understand..."

But he's not listening to me anymore. He's shaking his head, becoming smaller by the minute. He's leaving? I try to launch forward. To stop him, but I don't move. He's slipping back into the darkness.

Theodore! No! Don't leave me!

The flaring darkness doesn't last long as another voice stills my rambling.

"You promised me, Lee."

Though the timidly soft voice that always carries a large amount of strength lacks the cold tone Theo had, it doesn't stop my blood from freezing up. There's only one person I know with a voice as distinct as that. I search for the source of the voice, but all I'm faced with is complete darkness.

"Kalasiah?"

"You said you'll make it, you promised."

Her sobs suck in the silence in the dark and vibrate through me. I want to block it out, but I can't.

"Siah, stop!"

"No! You promised you wouldn't miss it! You promised it'd be the first thing you'll ever be early for. Everyone didn't believe you, but I did because I know you never promise things you don't mean."

The reminder plunges a hole into my already bleeding heart. My niece's first birthday.

"I want to make it too, Siah I really do, but..."

The sobbing ceases as quickly as it started, the grave silence taking over the air just before I feel a hand around my neck shutting off the air I'm breathing in.

I try to claw my fingers at her hand to get it off my windpipe but it is futile, just another useless attempt on my part.

Her blue-black afro is all up in my face as her ever soft mocha cat-like eyes stare at me coldly and glaring.

"S-iah," I gasp. "Y-o-ou'll ki-ill me."

"And what does it matter? You're ready to die anyway. What's bad in making it a tad bit quicker since you want to die so much?"

Anger flares up within me.

Why do they all think I want to give up so easily?

"I don't want to die, Siah, dammit!"

Strength radiates through me and I thrust the hand, choking me away from my neck, which leaves me wheezing for air. I glare up at her.

"Then fight you bitch! Who cares about luck? Stand up and fight for your freaking life."

Open your eyes and fight!

Fight!

Voices echo one after the other, with the word repeated over and over again.

I want to...but how can I?

My fists tighten, realizing all I was just about to do. Give up? No, that isn't me. Kalisha Morales isn't a quitter. I've never been one and I'm not going to start now.

I just... I hate blood.

WAKE UP AND FIGHT!

My eyes jerk open to a more familiar darkness and a coldness from the metallic floor that zaps through every feeling of heat in me. My mind is now alert and the echoes of Andres' laughter ring in my ears.

Not long has passed and I'm still alive.

Nausea swirls inside once I realize I'm still bleeding. There's a rush that almost consumes me to succumb back into the darkness but a memory holds me in place.

"Just listen for once, Lee! You never know when you'll need it."

"I won't ever be in a position to need that. Thank you very much, Rae."

She grunts and pushes me down onto a sit by the side. "Good, because I don't want you to, either, but IF you ever are there, then it's good to get the right first aid you need to stop the bleeding with how much you hate blood. So listen."

Turning away from her slightly, I nod. "You won't leave me until I do, would you?"

"Definitely not."

"Then, by all means, teach me how to stop,"- I grimace - "a bleeding wound."

Thank you, Rae.

I groan as I take in a deep breath.

I can do this.

My head is a bit hazy with the movement of trying to make myself comfortable.

Be careful, don't move suddenly. You can make the situation a lot worse if you do.

Andres moves in front of me, paying me little to no attention and that's all I need.

Thinking I could take him down first was a huge wrong on my part. Now that ship has sunk, I need to focus solely on not dying and getting out of here and I need to be fast. There's no saying what Andres is thinking.

You need a make-shift gauze. You can tear off a piece of cloth...

I look down at my top. This can work but tearing it. Andres is still distracted now but if I do that, his attention would be on him instantly. I can't afford that, not now, at least.

I suck in a huge amount of breath and brace up for the pain that I know is coming as I struggle to remove my top. Tears spill down my eyes but I stop them. I will do this. I have to. For Kalasiah. Anything for my sister.

Every part of me still feels the pressure of losing as much blood as I have but with my sister at the forefront of my mind, I push forward and tie the cloth to apply direct pressure to the wound, biting hard on my lips at the extra hurt it causes.

Once that is done, I take in a breath of relief to calm myself.

Now how do I get out of here?

Figure out where you are and what you know about the place.

Where am I?

I'm stuck in an elevator on floor 70.

What's unique about floor 70?

Nothing, it's the floor...

Oh shit.

My head whips to the logo by the side, forcing a sharp pain to shoot through me and my vision blurs up for a bit but none of it prevents the gasp that escapes my lips at the sight before me.

□ · □□□□□□ · ℕ · □□□□□□ · □

✎Word Count: 1581

✎Total Word Count: 7978

Vote, Comment, and Share if you enjoyed it!

□ · □□□□□□ · ₪ · □□□□□□ · □

□ · □□□□□□ · ℕ · □□□□□□ · □

□
NOTHING SCREAMS BEING at home like the constant whirring of wheels against the white marble floor and the blaring of electronics being worked on. Add the buzz of the city behind a clean glass and you get a freaking mansion.

And for that reason, I have my large mahogany table facing the glass window of our spacious office space despite the complaints of all my co-workers about it being unprofessional.

But I honestly think they're just all secretly jealous they didn't think about it first.

"Do you, need any help?" A dronish electronic voice asks by my side.

I turn with a smile to Astor. His green metallic eyes stay fixed on me and I know he's scanning my facial expression to know my answer. Tilting my head to the side, my smile increases, proud of my handwork. His gold ear tip band glows, a mark I give to all her customized robots that just makes me even more proud.

"And what do you think?" I ask him once the emerald green eyes turn to a lighter shade.

"I think, you're perfectly capable, of doing everything, by yourself because you're that good."

Someone scoffs from my other side, and I roll my eyes.

Jealousy, I tell you.

I don't turn around. I don't even have to turn to know that I'll receive a piercing glare from Charlotte's grey eyes with flashy gold streaks that shouldn't be glaring at people.

"Anyway," she says so loudly, I can't help the chuckle that escapes my lips. "Have you heard the rumors going on about floor 70?" she asks.

She sounds a lot closer than normal, seeing as her desk is on the other side of the office space. I turn slightly to the side and scoff at the sight before me.

Him? How can she want to gossip with him?

He raises his chiseled, sculptured face staring at her only for a moment. His eyes caries their everyday message of telling everyone to beat it and his lips are set in their regular straight line before he re-focuses on rearranging anything her bare presence by his desk may have disarranged, knowing he has passed his message across.

A man of paltry words and one after my heart. Just like me, he knows he's more than good enough and that's why his desk is even near mine. He's a lot more tolerable than the others in the long run.

I have no qualms with the rest of my team, but you can't get along perfectly with everyone. With Theodore, there's a quiet understanding between us. He thrives and knows it, except he doesn't make an extra effort to be good like I do.

But Charlotte unlike other times is determined to not receive the message. She continues staring at the top of his auburn sleek hair with sheer determination even though there's a slight flush on her porcelain skin as she raises her hand to touch her chocolate brown shoulder-length hair.

"This is a serious fact, Theo. Floor 70 is such a mysterious floor, even Kalisha doesn't know what goes on there."

"Rumors are not facts," Theo replies as a matter of fact with his cold, deep voice, not sparing her a glance.

His reply gets me out of the frozen state of my name being brought into the conversation and it seems I'm not the only one, as movement around the office space has stopped.

Yeah, that was unexpected.

"That's beside the point," Charlotte utters after recovering.

"But he, makes a good, point. Rumors are..."

"Oh shut it, Astor," Charlotte groans.

"Hey!" I spin fully to glare at her. No one touches my robots or speaks to them like that.

She stands defiant with a smile, ready to take me on, but a light, hearty voice interrupts any actions.

"You seem really set on this floor 70 rumor-fact. Why?" Emily asks, blinking her innocent sky-blue eyes at Charlotte.

Though I wonder why she asked since her laid-back rather than pressed-forward appearance speaks volumes of her lack of curiosity about the matter.

"Well, because it's a very interesting story. Have you ever noticed the sign on floor 70 when you're coming up to work?"

"I believe when you're coming up to work you should focus on work and not on the company sign that you probably see everywhere," Theodore says defiantly and turns to glare at her.

She's really making him uncomfortable.

"But it's different on the 70th floor!"

"Then, by all means, please tell us what is different, Char?" Emily says, rolling her eyes at Charlotte, who perks up at the question.

"So, on floor 70." Her voice drips but booms with excitement.

Despite every other person being unnecessarily concerned, the robots around stop wheeling, looking at her ready and eager to garner a new bit of information to add to their repertoire of info.

"I hear the V is turned upside down."

Now, this grabs my attention. "I'm sorry?"

"Yes, you heard right, Kalisha." Charlotte turns to me with a smug look. "It looks exactly like the 'a' before it. The juicy part is if you notice that and you push the letters a, t, l & e, another door entirely would open. Apparently, it's the ONLY way to get into the 70th floor."

Emily is the first person to scoff and return to her workplace as do a lot of other robots including Astor. Theodore spares her no glance, grunting and re-arranging his things on his table. Most likely pissed, he even gave her his attention.

"I'm serious!"

"Oh, darling." I take my moment, shaking my head at her with a smile plastered on my lips. "Has making robots become such a bore to you? You now intend to live in the fantasy world?"

"To live, in a fantasy world, you need to be, a lot more creative," Astor says eliciting a giggle from every other person.

I wink at him, laughing as Charlotte fumes, looking at everyone.

"You would need it sometime when you're stuck in an elevator and then you'll come to thank me!" she huffs.

"No one would need it, Charlotte. Thanks to Kalisha, who has put procedures in place for when one gets stuck in the elevator. So, why don't you instead go back to your desk and, you know, get creative," Theodore says and a burst of laughter reverberates around the room.

It really looks like I need them now, doesn't it?

I really hope for once that your rumors are very real, Charlotte.

Right now, they actually seem real. The letters that spelled Shaveal Robotics Limited rest on the wall but unlike how it does so perfectly on all other floors, the letter V on this floor is upside down.

I stand up but I hiss painfully at the way I do. Unfortunately, this doesn't happen as silently as I really wished I did.

Andres spins around to face me so fast, probably shocked that I am standing, but I don't wait for him to make a move. I continue on to my mission to the letters.

Getting to the front of the sign, I take a deep breath.

Charlotte, my life depends on your words now. It better be true.

I tug at letters A in Shaveal, letter T in robotics, and E and L in limited right after each other, holding my breath and hoping that there is no arrangement to this twist.

"What do you think you're doing?!" Andres growls right behind me.

I spin around to face him with my heart in my chest, but everything stops.

A screeching grunt of the metal shifting behind echoes, zapping away the frightening silence Andres.

It's over. It's finally over. I'm free.

Andres contorts into a fit of anger, which I should expect but there's a hint of a crooked smile that makes my heart skip, and then it all happens so fast.

The elevator gives a sudden jerk. There's a squeak from below, out of the elevator.

Air swoops into the elevator as the floor gives way.

□ · □□□□□□ · ₪ · □□□□□□ · □

✎WORD COUNT: 1353

✎TOTAL WORD COUNT: 9331

Vote, Comment, and Share if you enjoyed it!

□ · □□□□□□ · ₪ · □□□□□□ · □

☐ · ☐☐☐☐☐☐ · ₪ · ☐☐☐☐☐☐ · ☐

Whoosh!

A shrill scream explodes from my lips in a fierce battle with the clang and clink of the metal crashing against the wall as the floor falls down through the space.

My body shakes in a violent terror and my hands grip the railing so hard I'm sure my knuckles are turning white. I watch everything I own chase after the floor with Andres in hot pursuit.

My scream fades with the intensity of the sound of the crashing of the floor. The vast hollow beneath my dangling feet sucks up my racing heartbeat.

I continue staring with wide eyes and an open mouth until the final clang burst out vibrating through the place from the impact, causing me to shudder.

There's no screaming beneath or any other sound that would show Andres' fate, but I know no one can survive a fall like that. It's freaking 70 floors distance, after all.

Sweat builds up in my hand from the tightness of my hold and it suddenly feels slippery against the metal. This pulls my attention away from the fall. Slowing down my breaths, I peel off one hand after another, drying it on the cloth. I can't afford to fall, not after everything.

There's just one question plaguing my thoughts. Just how did an elevator floor separate from the rest of its body?

My hands slip again and I tuck the question to the back of my mind, focusing on getting myself out of this first. I tighten my hands on the railing and pain shoots sharply through my body as my muscles scream in protest, but I gulp it down, knowing what I have to do.

Thankfully, years of visiting the gym and doing this exercise prepare me for this. But the ease I have come accustomed to in the gym is lost in transition by the pain already crawling in my body.

I slowly take in a deep breath, closing my eyes for a brief second before I hurl myself instantly, groaning deeply at the sharp pain that pierces through my body.

Tears pool in my eyes but I hold it all in resting my knees on the railing. The searing cold from the pressure on my knees is not welcome at all.

A slight gasp escapes my lips once my sweaty feet almost slip off. I try to take it slow, breathing and trying to calm myself down.

Once I settle myself within and on the railing, I push myself upwards towards this opening. Grunting at each push, I land past the opened door onto a cold white titled floor.

My knees buckle beneath me but I don't care. My entire body shakes terribly as the tears fall non-stop from my eyes. It's over. With my head bent down, a burst of shaky laughter escapes my lips from just appreciating the white floor and the bright light that engulfs me.

I collapse onto the floor, lying flat taking deep breaths to settle my racing heart and give my aching muscles time to relax before I look up, ready to find a permanent way out of this.

The drop of that elevator would have got attention, hopefully, there's already help on its way. I'm going to need it.

Though, hasn't anyone seen me? Why haven't they rushed forward wondering what is going on?

I turn around, lying on my chest instead to face my front.

The emptiness of the floor slaps me in the face forcing me to sit up. Rather than a small corridor leading to a big office space with desks, people, and robots, I face a long narrow corridor with doors on each side, like a prison with jail rooms that have metal doors and not burglary doors.

For a company with 76 floors, every floor has to be unique in its own way, but this makes my blood run cold. It's different, too different from any other floor I've been on, and that sets my heart ablaze.

Something is wrong. From the special opening to this floor to this, there's just something I can't put my hands on. What was Haveal thinking? What am I missing?

There is the difference in the floor that throws my relief at getting away from Andres into the sea and the graveyard silence in the corridor drowns it.

I... I thought I will be able to ask someone for help but the silence mocks my thoughts. There's no one here, and that is wrong.

I crawl to the wall, placing my hands on it and pushing my entire weight on it, my breaths go in and out at a fast pace.

My gaze darts back and forth with my brows furrowed, trying to make sense of everything.

I flinch the moment a static shrill slice into my thoughts. Whipping my head in the sound's direction brings me face to face with sound systems attached to the rear end corners of the corridor.

What was...

Just like before by thoughts are interrupted by rattling, making me turn again back to the space where the elevator used to be.

It's coming from there.

My chest tightens as the sound gets louder, but I don't have to wonder for long what is going on as the peach-coloured calloused hand that stopped the elevator doors for me slams against the tiled floor. A resounding clack from the crushed tile beneath his hand follows this action.

I gulp hard, staring wide-eyed at the action.

What the...

I stagger backward, staring at him. How is he here? The elevator floor fell 70 floors for goodness sake! No one should survive that impact, or recover quick enough to save their selves and still make it back up.

No one, no living human being. No human...

I stop short as a scoff escapes my lips. Human. How did I miss that?

With both hands on the floor, his face comes into view.

My breath halts and I slowly, with no strength, raise my head up to see what is going on.

The eyes that I thought looked lifeless compared to a human's regular ones just because he may have been a creepy fellow now make all the sense in the world.

Chills grip my body, and my stomach tightens.

It can't be, right? H- He c-ca-an't be.

There's no way. We've never made one who looked like a human. There's no...

But who am I kidding?

The reducing of the icy blue iris staring at me, an action of concentration foreign to humans, tells me all I need to know.

Andres is not a human but a carefully made robot.

□ · □□□□□□ · ₪ · □□□□□□ · □

✎ WORD COUNT: 1,106

✎ TOTAL WORD COUNT: 10,437

Vote, Comment, and Share if you enjoyed it!

□ · □□□□□□ · ₪ · □□□□□□ · □

□ · □□□□□□ · ₪ · □□□□□□ · □

JUST AS EVERYTHING makes sense, it also doesn't. That sentence fills my mind with a whirlwind of images that torment my sanity. Am I meant to be glad he isn't some creepy human with hatred boiling within him for me or sad because I'm being tortured by the one thing I've spent most of my life making?

The brightly lit room suddenly feels small, and it's like I'm back in the elevator's darkness, losing my breath and my blood.

A brassy sharp noise emits from the loudspeaker at the corners of the corridor. My hands' raise to protect my ears from the gravitating sound and they freeze up in that position along with the rest of my body.

"You didn't think this was over, did you?"

I spring up as my heart races, almost exploding. My feet wobble at the sudden movement, crashing me back down, but I grip the wall beside me to keep myself on my feet.

What is happening here?

Time halts, or at least I think it does as he comes up for a better view. With his hands first and then his head that gives me the ultimate confirmation, if I ever need one, of its robotic lineage.

His eyes zoom in on me, the light reflects in it and it feels like there's an electric spark that connects his eyes to my body. A chill seizes me, making me want nothing more than for the earth to swallow me whole.

With an awkward smirk plastered on his face, he looks at me holding knowledge that I'm not privileged to have. He uses his hands to propel his self upwards at a speed that contrasts the way time slows down for me, whilst I try to understand what is going on.

Knots form in the throat as I take it in fully.

Yes, he still has the body build of Andres, but that is it. The peach skin is long gone as it peeled off the moment he landed on the floor and in its place are smooth silver metals running along every part of its body.

"Surprise!" The metallic voice rings through the corridor, rattling my core.

I have heard robots speak so many times I can't keep count, but there's everything different about the way he speaks that makes tiny, slimy, invisible insects crawl over the entirety of my body.

It's dronish but cold and full of hatred.

As he moves just ever so slightly, I'm stunned in place as right there on his left ear is something that is familiar, too familiar.

Whirring of wheels against the floor, murmuring and hitting of metals fill the office space, but I'm focused on the work of art in front of me.

I put an earpiece made specifically for him in place and take a step back admiring my work with a full-blown smile.

As silence follows this simple act, the hairs on my body twitch and I know that all my co-workers are staring at me from their cubicles.

"Keep the jealousy in check, guys. It would make him crumble," I snicker at them, not looking back.

"Don't get ahead of yourself, Lee. No one is jealous here," Theodore says as a matter of fact and I can't do anything to hold back the grin that pops on my face because we both know how true my statement is for everyone except him.

"Right?" Daren, the youngest member of our team who has as much enthusiasm as the black curls in his hair, agrees, popping to my side to inspect the robot with me.

He stretches his hands to touch it, and I smack it away before he can even try.

"What the hell, dude?" he groans, glaring at me.

"Do not touch," I sneer.

"Is it so wrong to be curious for once? I just want to know why you put the blue earpiece. It stands out too much, even for you."

I smile at the finishing touch I added. My hands glide over it with my heart swelling. "I just wanted that resemblance to a part of myself so when I see it anywhere, I'd know it's mine."

I'd know it's mine.

I stifle staring straight at the glacial blue earpiece.

"You." I shudder as I spit the words out of my mouth, though it's barely audible.

How can this even be true? I didn't create a murderer. Far from it, really. He solved every problem, not this...

A gravitating squeaky noise escapes his lips.

Is that- is that meant to be a chuckle?

"You recognize me, now? Wow, took you long enough, mother."

I stumble backward a bit, shaking my head.

It can't be. How can this, this monstrous atrocity be a creation of mine?

Mother? I may have programmed it, built him to look like this, but I did not mean him to call me mother or be anything like this. No, he was my best piece yet, my pride. The one who I should have auctioned off at the presentation today.

Metallic scraping cuts through my thoughts and I look back to Andres, who the sound is coming from and I sputter watching it transform even further.

Weapons sprout out in place of his hands and arms.

I can't even think as I watch it continue unfolding. Each transformation slices through a part of my heart, watching something I've put a lot of work into becoming something else.

Tears pool in my eyes as I recognize every crazy idea jotted down in the corners of my books just for the fun of my crazy head. It feels nothing less than surreal watching stupid notes coming to life right in front of me.

I choke back the disbelieving tears once it's done. There's nothing recognizing able about Andres anymore. No. It looks just like a metallic body used to store weapons by people who care less about their properties.

"Perfect. Human skin was a great suppressor of my full potential. How do I look, mother?"

Terrible, like a freaking murderer, and a filthy experiment gone wrong.

The words are strong in my mind and heart, but that's where the peak of their strength is as they make it past my lips. The way it slurs the name mother with its robotic voice irks me so badly, that I can't say anything.

But my lack of reply doesn't faze him, rather it encourages him to keep talking.

"If you like how I look, you should totally check out my friends."

Friends?! There are more of him?

My pulse takes a sudden quick pace at his words and I know it reflects the feeling in my wide eyes which causes his own to show a tingle of excitement flowing through them.

"They are lovely," he added.

Instantly, there's screeching and rattling of metallic bodies against each other and these bodies hop into the corridor right by Andres' side from the opened space where he came in from.

I take a startled step back as they keep pouring into the corridor.

There are different parts of a robot, the lower body without a head, the upper part without hands, and just any part that was discarded or safely kept aside for future use. They stand there with weapons edged callously into different parts of their incomplete body.

This is just horrible.

I stare at Andres with my eyebrows scrunched up, pulled together, and my eyes tense. There's an urge to ask him what he had done, how he did it, and why he is doing it, but from the robotic crooked smile that makes its way to his lips, I instantly know this is no time to ask questions.

His little minions seem to whir up instantly, getting ready.

I turn around promptly just as the mini-robots scratch against each other, pushing in my direction, ready to attack.

That will not happen.

I'm in a corridor filled with doors. There's got to be a way out of here. I dash to the first door with a mind to be ready for about anything.

The clicking of the door releases the breath I didn't even realize I was holding, but I'm not surprised I was. Wasting no time to bathe in my relief, I turn the handle all the way down, pushing the door open.

I spring backward at a speed familiar to Olympic winners, shutting the door back with a screech that pushes itself out of my lips.

My hands rush like the waves of the sea to my aching back, trying to soothe the pain searing in me.

A burning smell wafts through the air after swirling my breathing into a fast, distorted rhythm.

Something burnt me, tearing through my clothes and causing a mark on my skin. With my eyes opened wide and my jumbled thoughts, nothing makes sense again.

I'm looking right at an empty long corridor that should easily be a free passageway away from the robots behind me, but something there burnt through my skin keeping me in place.

A robotic disapproving sound from Andres spins my attention o him. He's shaking his head at me but still has a smile on with his mob right by him.

He knows what is keeping me in place. Of course he does.

"Running away, mother? That's not fair. The game is just about to begin."

I gulp hard, staring at him. Being back here at the point of my insides sinking low and energy-draining from not knowing where to go from here or what to do makes my skin crawl. It is like a never-ending cycle I can't seem to get out of.

But how does one escape from being stuck in between invisible laser beams and zombie robots?

□ · □□□□□□ · ₪ · □□□□□□ · □

✎Word Count: 1,629

✎Total Word Count: 12,066

Vote, Comment, and Share if you enjoyed it!

□ · □□□□□□ · ₪ · □□□□□□ · □

□ · □□□□□□ · ₪ · □□□□□□ · □

█ SWEAT TRICKLES DOWN my body with no regard for the further discomfort it causes me.

Why?

I can barely recognize myself right now as for the first time in a while I feel so weak and I don't care anymore. I just- I just want someone to save me from this never-ending misery. Why is there no one to help me?!

The slight constricted pain from self-pity doesn't last long with Andres taking a fight pose that puts my pity state to a stop.

Oh, shoot!

"Ready or not, here we come!"

That is all the warning I get before the robots launch themselves at me. I gulp down my saliva hard and stumble backwards, hitting an activated laser beam.

"Please!" I whimper. The plea cracks from my lips before I can put a stop to it. My voice comes out cracked and so foreign. It's piercing.

The pungent burning smell drifts through the air.

I bite hard on my lips, tasting my blood, and thrust forward on instinct, straight into an incoming knife of one robot. It cuts through the skin on my lap making me grunt sharply, but with my immediate reaction of flinging my hands at it, tossing it aside, the knife doesn't go any deeper.

Instead, it crashes against the wall, shattering into pieces. This pushes the others forward even more.

My description of them fits. Zombies. With no care in the world.

Pain stings in my eyes with a voracity that causes my body to tremble, but that does not get me a break. A small hand holding a long knife comes straight for my toes. I snatch it from the floor, hoping to use the weapon as my own. It struggles against my hand, cutting into my flesh and causing droplets of blood to spill onto the floor. Shoot!

My ribs squeeze in and I lose the act of breathing. My body feels hot, dangerously ready to burst out and evaporate through thin air, but I can't get a breather as they keep coming one after another, intent on finishing the job they started or in their terms the game they started.

With my heavy, flaring hands, I swing some robots to the laser beams behind me as they get close to me.

Andres grunts and I instantly know he's angry that I could even overpower any of the robots. That would make the aim of this futile, I'm guessing.

At the sound of his grunt, the robots change course and instead of coming one at a time, they charge forward together, their distinct weapons stretched towards me and clashing against each other.

Andres launches one robot past the others on the ground straight at me. I twist to my left to evade the incoming robot, but that sprouts a wrong decision on my part. The tightened cloth around my waist soaks up more blood as my twist disturbed the imperfect wrap.

My eyes sting even more matching each clash of weapons against my skin with some of the robots getting attached and unable to detach themselves. They are just body parts themselves, after all.

At every inch of me, the disastrous dark red liquid oozes out, taking with it the strength that I need right now as well as my oxygen.

I can't- can't keep fighting them off. How do they just keep- keep increasing?! Even with the mass of unmoving robots at my feet, there is still so much more trying to reach me.

I look straight ahead to the one who's standing still, enjoying the scene by the side. The whole thing comes down to him and him alone. After all, it all started with him.

Knowing that pushing all these mini-robots to me doing nothing himself is to weaken me, so he gets the last blow. This means without them in the way, I stand a chance to end things.

What on earth can I do right now? How do I make sure I don't die here? Just what have I been overlooking?

Andres is meant to be mine, a part of my creation. That- That just means I should have a remote to keep him in check safely kept...

Right. In my bag that is down with the rest of the shattered elevator floor pieces.

Of course. Of course, the solution to all this would be far from my reach. What in its right senses would let the solution to its prey's suffering be handed on a platter? I'm sure that's why it sent the floor crashing down. Scare her up a bit but also take from her only resolution.

A strangled groan pours out of my lips as a knife is driven into my side, all thanks to my distracted thoughts. I crumble to the floor with tears spilling down my eyes.

Can't it all just stop?! Why can't time just freaking stop for one stupid moment, stopping with it all the pain and fatigue stirring through my body right now?

Everything blurs out thanks to the tears and my head wants to fall off with its lack of weight.

There's no part of me that wants to continue this fight, but how can I stop now? After losing this much blood and pushing through to this stage. But even if I want to push on, what do I do? What can a weak person like me possibly do to get herself out of this freaking mess?

I want to take my time to think, to scrape the barrels of my supposedly big brain and come up with an idea but with each time spent thinking, a double dose of pain erupts through my body.

With it all, I try to multi-task. I take a deep breath in, flinging another robot that comes at me. My skin tingles continuously. The dripping of sweat adds to the sketchy feeling growing in me.

I grunt at the back of my throat in irritation, throwing another one.

The outright plan had been to control Andres with a remote, but I put a Plan B in place for my robot and every other functioning robot in this place.

The end to all this would be in... The freaking control room.

My eyes flicker around the room whilst I avoid an incoming foreign piercing object from a robot and stop short at the sight of a blinking red light from a CCTV camera just ahead of the laser beams, but trained directly at me.

I turn from it to a robot coming at me and for the first time take in its zombie movements. Yes, I called them zombies from the onset, but it just didn't click that they were being controlled like that.

Just like lifeless puppets with invisible ropes directing their every movement. I just thought they were purposefully made creations from whatever just for torturing me because every robot created in Shaveal has the first operation to walk properly.

I swirl to face Andres and my eyes widen, watching him watch me and not the robots.

How could I have missed it?

My eyes cloud up as I feel wheels turning at a faster rate in my head.

Andres isn't controlling himself or in control of the robots. Some-one is doing this.

Yes, this should have been clear from the beginning if this would not be a case of my robot doing dark by itself and turning on me. But the reality that someone has been sitting behind the computer watching me get beaten and almost lose my life makes my blood boil.

What in the freaking hell is wrong with people?!

□ · □□□□□□ · ₪ · □□□□□□ · □

✎Word Count: 1,272

✎Total Word Count: 13,338

Vote, Comment, and Share if you enjoyed it!

□ · □□□□□□ · ₪ · □□□□□□ · □

□ · □□□□□ · ℕ · □□□□□ · □

◻ SOMETIMES FINDING A SOLUTION to a problem doesn't always mean you find the peace you search for. Knowing that someone is enjoying just because I am hurt and bleeding lets chills creep up on each path of my body, taking its precious time.

It only draws me back to the fact that Andres called me Kali. For a minute, I think it's him and I just can't breathe, but it can't be him. He is meant to spend the rest of his life there, so he can't be anywhere near me.

This conclusion just makes me want to figure out who this clueless bastard is. No one messes with me like this and gets away with it.

But looking at the mess going on around me, I can't help the heat that flushes through my body and my vein twitches.

Why would anyone decide to use everything everyone in this company worked so hard on just to what? See me dead? For what stupid reason? I might seem like a broken record trying to ask what I could do to deserve such a thing, but no matter how cocky I am, I don't think I could have hurt anyone so much they'd want me dead.

There's a continuous pounding in my ear and a spring of unpleasant words sprout from my lips. I'm suddenly a ticking bomb as I grab hold of the next robot coming at me and hurl it straight at the CCTV.

The crash of the two objects fills the room, and an instant silence prevails.

"What have you done?!"

The question scrapes against my skin, pushing out ridiculous goosebumps from it whilst sending shocking waves through me, choking me. But I don't let myself wallow in that feeling; instead, I toss it aside and let a lighter feeling find its way through my body.

It worked, and that's all that matters. If he can't see me now, maybe that changes things. I glare at Andres, holding myself up high, glaring at him with all that I have. "What I should have done a long time ago?" I growl out. I tighten my fist and surge towards with no calculation insight.

Combining all my jumbled thoughts, I sense the mistakes taking irrational steps would cause, but I can't seem to give myself time to think things through before taking action. So I push on forward.

With the mini-robots attacking each other and not focusing on me, thanks to their lack of sight, I use the opportunity to snatch one knife detached from a robot.

Andres' attention zeros in on me, instantly sensing the change in me from a mile away.

That right there is something that I programmed into him. This piece of information hits me, shattering my heart into even more tiny pieces.

We move immediately and our blades brush against each other. The force I use for each counterattack is no match for his as he sends me stumbling backward at each strike, each adding a more painful sizzling ache to my opened wounds than the last.

My hands feel like a freaking bag of cement placed on a single weightless coin. But with every clash of weapons and every production of a new weapon, I come to the further realization that it is not mine. I may have started it, but someone else took over.

Someone, for whatever reason, is leeching off my work. I would not let just anyone to do that and get away with it. Not while I'm still breathing even if the breaths are failing me.

Silence prevails as the crashing of robots against each other ceases. Whoever, whether it is one person or a group of people up there, has poured all the attention into just one robot.

Andres.

"You're only hurting yourself, mother." Andres squeaks as he incites another slash on my body. My breath shudders with the burn I feel.

I stagger backward, tightening my muscles, hoping to stay still and put just a bit of distance between us. I raise my head up high with my eyes reflecting the coldness he had at the beginning.

"You are no creation of mine," I snarl.

I snag a knife from his leg, breaking it off. That, along with the other knife in my possession, I cut off its leg, setting the wires within it free.

A grating growl radiates from it as he crumbles down on his knees, but it's still moving.

"I am your creation!" it growls out. It pushes forward, swinging a knife, but at no precise movement. "Everything, right from the start, began because of you. You created the robot, me. You designed this situation, forged the story and started the game. It was all you, mother."

I falter in my steps with my face scrunched up.

"What does that- what are you saying?"

No! No! No! I cannot let myself be fooled by this nonsense. I will not let it happen.

I push forward with that final decision edged into my head, snatch a knife from the side, and plunge it right into the gaping hole created by the earpiece.

Incoherent words sputter from its lips as it crashes down onto the floor in a resounding crash. A free breath pushes out of my mouth, with my body feeling lighter.

"Then I will end the story."

□ · □□□□□□ · ℕ · □□□□□□ · □

✎ WORD COUNT: 892

✎ TOTAL WORD COUNT: 14,230

Vote, Comment, and Share if you enjoyed it!

□ · □□□□□□ · ℕ · □□□□□□ · □

°1 11 1°

□ · □□□□□ · ₪ · □□□□□ · □

ONE WOULD THINK it is all over, but it isn't. Knowing that the main reason I'm battered and covered in bruises is in the control room is all I let myself think about. I have to get there before the person runs away.

My eyes get cloudy as darkness threatens to take over. Letting the image of the control room and a silhouette of who I want to face fill the forefront of my mind is what I do to not give in to the darkness.

I need to find out who did this to me and why they felt the need to do this.

There's no time to prevent all the wounds from bleeding so I don't even think about it. I grunt, lifting myself up from the ground with a robotic hand I snatch up by my right side.

After what feels like an eternity, I stand up to my full length. My legs wobble beneath me and I stumble against the wall to keep me standing.

I must do this!

Looking around, I shudder at the sight of blood on the white walls alongside scratches from the strength of robots hitting it.

I shut my eyes instantly before I feel like throwing up and get distracted from where I need to go.

Of course, with the amount of blood I have lost, I have so little strength left in me. The question of if I can make it pops into my head as uncertainty makes its way into my mind.

I may not make it to the end but I know that if I fail without trying, whatever afterlife I go on to, I'll hate myself and that's something I don't want.

The control room is on the seventy-second floor. My eyes flutter open and flicker to the elevator or the shadow of it.

Yeah, that can't work.

The idea drowns as quickly as it floated up. The only other option is the stairs. Tears flow down my eyes at the thought of having to climb up the stairs in my weakened state and anger fuels me.

How did I become such a mess?

I stagger backwards the moment my eyes flicker to Andres on the floor. The promise of who he was and what he represented sank my heart into the flood of who he is now and what they made of him.

Andres. No, his name was Garv, my symbol of pride. He was meant to be everything to everyone who got to use him because I made him to make them feel protected and good about themselves. But now he's been reduced to a couple of messy parts on the floor and this was done with nothing but my hands.

I don't look at my hands, knowing my resolve will crumble instantly.

With the shift in my priority, I focus solely on the anger building up for whoever turned me into this mess.

Thanks to my heart pounding, I channel the adrenaline pouring into my nerves from that one emotion and pull myself straight up. Once I'm up, I take in deep, slow breaths, staring at the scene before me, ready to take my next step.

There's a slightly ajar door which I'm assuming opened from the pressure of a robot I threw off of me during the fight. The door which leads right to the staircase I need.

This might be just another plan from my perpetrator, but the fact I have settled on finding the staircase, I can help the sudden giddiness flowing through me.

Though it pans out quite fast realizing that finding the door to the stairs is one thing and getting to it is another.

The broken pieces of robots on the floor and the freaking invisible lasers feel like two peas in a poisonous pod for me right now, but the best thing about poison is that you get to pick how it affects you, right?

I'm just going to use one poison to conquer the other one.

I grab hold of discarded robots at each turn to move around the laser beams. I throw them at different angles to get a sense of where each laser beam is. Once a robot hits a laser beam, it burns through, letting the pungent smell of fire flow through the room. The test run helps me get to the door with no burn.

But my breath goes in laboured and harsh once I'm there. Locking my eyes on the door across from me, my hand tightens on the robotic hand. I think about the nameless individual who would go to such lengths to hurt me this badly.

I take in a deep purposeful breath and stumble across the slightly opened door, but my legs fail me and I crash onto the floor.

I release a sharp cry of agony at the pressure of hitting the floor. My eyes sting and the stairs before me suddenly feel like a mountain with rigid edges that are impossible to climb.

Dragging myself across each step seems like the best option right now. Conserve energy before I get to the person who would require all the energy in me to attack.

I move, one hand at a time, though I groan, unable to ignore the sting I feel from each movement I make, but I don't stop. Since I have come this far, I'm going to just have to keep moving on.

"Now, this is such a disgraceful sight for sore eyes." The deep, intense voice breaks into my movement. There's a familiarity to the tone that stiffens me.

"Never in a million years would I have thought I'd see the great Kalisha Morales look so pitiful and unsightly," he continues.

My ears ring once my brain places the voice to the rightful owner.

It can't- it just can't be. I don't feel like moving anymore. I don't want to face the person anymore.

Resting my back against the wall behind me, my head moves on instinct despite not wanting to confirm it. Nothing I want changes the person on who I set my opened wide eyes on.

Just a floor above me is confirming my present suspicion. He stands with his tall and lanky form, putting pressure on his slim ivory hands that rest on the staircase railing, staring at me with his olive-green eyes and his narrow lips pulled into a sinister smile.

"Haveal?"

□ · □□□□□□ · ₪ · □□□□□□ · □

✎Word Count: 1,072

✎Total Word Count: 15,302

Vote, Comment, and Share if you enjoyed it!

□ · □□□□□□ · ₪ · □□□□□□ · □

▢ · □□□□□ · ₪ · □□□□□ · □

◻ BETTER THE DEVIL you know than the angel you don't, people say.

Sitting right here in this situation, I finally understand what they are talking about.

I dreaded seeing him here, but somehow looking at Haveal Campbell, the CEO of Shaveal Robotics Limited, I actually wish it was him instead.

I'm appalled by his presence, but what gets me is the scowl on his face, a scowl that worked so well on the rest of my co-workers when they slacked off or didn't meet up the quota in ways he wanted.

But even as I stare at such a familiar look on a familiar face, I ward off unbelievable thoughts from my mind. My mouth goes dry as I shake my head vigorously, not coming to terms with what my eyes are seeing. There must be a misunderstanding somewhere. There has to be.

"Haveal? What's going on? Are you alright? Do you know what's going on here?"

Though the questions spill from my mouth, with the way my chest constricts and the knowing look on his face, I have my answer, but I just can't bring myself to believe it.

Sure, he's known as the person who can bring hell to earth, but that's for work not torturing someone, definitely not that. He's not that type of person, right?"

"Come on, I know you are smarter than this. You made the robot that was about to be auctioned out to protect and secure important officials and help in military strategies. There's no way you can't figure out what is going on. Don't bring shame to this company now, Kalisha. Not when you've been doing good for yourself."

His words cut through the rest of my body that's not wounded, leaving me bleeding out. I press my palm over my mouth, staring at him with a clouded vision just before I release a shaky breath, letting my hand fall away.

"It... it was you?" I choke out.

He smirks, and the knowing look in his eyes wards off my disbelief like a fly escaping death.

"How could you?" I spit out the venom laced in my voice.

How could Haveal, who put so much love and priority on his robots more than anyone in this company, turn them into weapons of destruction? What could come over him?

He straightens up from his resting position on the railing and walks down the stairs with a grace that mocks my battered state.

"How couldn't I?" He says just as he reaches me.

I try to stand up from my crouched position, but it takes all the strength in me and so I collapse right back. The bleeding I had previously stopped in the elevator, opens up again.

"It is running out so soon?"

My knuckle muscles tear at each other at the fierceness of my tightened fist. I shake with anger at his nonchalant attitude about everything he's done to me. This isn't just about a bunch of stupid robots; it's about my freaking life.

"What the hell is wrong with you? You put my life at risk, you bastard. My life! Was this all just a game to you? Was that it? You were so bored, you just had to mess up someone's life?"

He scoffs with the edge of his pinched lips curving up. "I'd have called it a simulation of sorts, but a game?" He rubs his hands back and forth on his chin, his eyes looking inward as he nods. "It has a nice ring to it, don't you think?"

"You bastard!"

"Easy with the name-calling now. I just wanted to see to what extent you'd live up to your name. Kalisha," he says, having a feel of my name that causes me to want to puke. "Besides, didn't Andres already tell you?" he continues. "You started this game yourself."

"Wh... Started what? What the hell are you on about, huh? What bullshit are you spewing and what does that even have to do with your apparent freaking obsession with what a name means and who is living up to it? Why do you care?"

The calm aura he held on to previously, evaporates into thin air at my question. His hold laid-back gaze turns into a glare as he shouts, "Everything! It has everything to do with it and I just hate it. I hate everything about someone living up to their name."

Cold sweat breaks out from the change in the atmosphere. I reach out for the robotic hand by the side whilst keeping my steady gaze locked on him. With my body failing me, I can only question him like this, but I will have to be ready for when the time is right to act.

He doesn't notice this as he's lost in an angry world. He paces, sending me a glare at each point of his speech.

I would not go down alone.

"I hate every bit of it! Why would a mother give birth to a son and name him Haveal? Haveal; weak and small. Just because he doesn't exhibit the same strength as his brother, whom she named Henrick?

The insolence to think that because I was born smaller, that I would be weak throughout, needing help in everything, would be weak and weary. And somehow that's no problem because you were born that way." He scoffs.

"No! You see, I didn't live up to my name, no! I did the opposite. I would not be weak and I so strived to become what they least ex-pected. Became better than the so-called powerful brother, I became the youngest CEO of a robotics company with none of their measly help!" He puffs his chest out with a proud gleam in his eyes.

I blink rapidly, arching an eyebrow up.

What the hell does that have to do with me?

I choke back the question the moment he suddenly crouches down, so he's looking me in the eye. He grabs hold of my chin and raises it up forcefully, eliciting a groan from my lips.

I gulp hard at the chill in his eyes, but I do nothing, which is all the nudge he needs to keep talking.

"And then you came along. You never really started out flaunting your work. You were just someone who was good with whatever you did and knew it, and did I love that about you? Oh, I did. And when I told you, what did you say to me?!"

No! No way.

"'Lucky girls like me don't date bosses like you, Haveal.' Lucky girls who could get any man don't date weak men like me, was that it? Well, I bet you liked Andres then, the strong and manly man, just like his name means." A sinister smile pops onto his lips.

That's it?! That's the reason you'd put my life on the line, something that has happened a year ago?

My face scrunches up in disgust. You've got to be kidding me.

Muscles quivering and all, I swing the metal hand I'm holding before I think and hit him straight on his head.

He staggers away from me, his hold on my face loosening, but only for just a bit. He's quick enough to grab me as he stumbles back and lets us crash against the railing. Him first, and then I. Stars burst behind my eyelids as I try to manoeuvre away from the force, only to head straight for the hard floor.

Curses spew from his lips while his blurred silhouette gets up from his position, but I latch onto him.

Not this time. If I'm going to hell, I'm taking you down with me.

"If this is what you resort to because of a simple rejection, then you deserve the name your mother gave you. You freaking weak bastard."

I snatch the hand from the side and hit him with it. Blood boozes from the dash it causes and I suddenly feel elated. One strike after another and I don't want to stop.

"How. Can. You. Say. You. Liked. Me. And. Then. Want. To. Destroy. My. Life. Like. That?!" I shout through each hit, though I don't expect an answer from him. Blood splashes around with every hit but it doesn't even affect but rather spurs me on, seeing the light previously in his eyes fade away.

Even as life is slipping from his eyes, he smirks up at me, stopping me for a moment.

"Sound familiar?" he says just before I land the final blow and he goes limb beneath me.

I collapse by the side of him, finally letting all the exhaustion I've felt rain down on me, but it doesn't stop his last word from ringing continuously in my head even as darkness clouds my vision.

□ · □□□□□□ · ₪ · □□□□□□ · □

✎Word Count: 1,469

✎Total Word Count: 16,771

Vote, Comment, and Share if you enjoyed it!

□ · □□□□□□ · ₪ · □□□□□□ · □

□ · □□□□□ · ₪ · □□□□□ · □

SOUND FAMILIAR?

Kalisha! You said you like me, don't destroy my life like this!

"U- un- uncle- Uncle Aiden?"

"Uncle Aiden! Uncle Aiden, come on, let's go! They'll finish up soon!" My little cherry voice bounces off against the walls of the room as I run forward to drag my uncle.

He's promised to take me and just me to see the latest Disney musical show and I'm so excited!

He laughs, throwing his head back like he always does, letting his black coils bounce as he does so.

"Slow down there, Kali. We'll meet up. I'll make sure of it."

A smile brightens up my face, but I don't stop pulling him towards the door. He keeps his promises; I know that, but we can't afford to be late for this!

"Lee? Uncle Aiden?" Kalasiah calls out, stopping us from heading out the door. I turn, placing my hands on my waist, hoping she's not up to what I think she is.

Kalasiah stands up from the living room couch and makes her way to us. "Are you going already?" Excitement rises in her voice, all numbness from her sleep gone with the wind. "Can I ..."

"No!" I instantly say. "It's my day."

The light in her eyes goes down and she frowns. "Don't be stingy."

"I'm not stingy. You're just jealous." I stick out my tongue at her and pull Uncle Aiden before he can succumb to her request.

Uncle Aiden chuckles, ruffling up my hair. "You want me to yourself, don't you, Kali?" He says and I hide my face away from him with a smile on my lips and a definite flush on my cheeks.

It is true. All the time I spend with Uncle Aiden is my precious moment. I like how he takes time out of his busy moment to give me a surprise present even when it's not my birthday or takes me to watch a movie or in this case takes me to see the latest Disney musical show.

He laughs again, lifting my spirits. "Anything for my enchanting lucky charm."

· ₪ ·

It's movie night and mom and dad are around, but that's not the exciting part. Uncle Aiden is around too! Dad says he needs a break from work and that's why he's here. It's really not any of my business. I'm just happy he's here!

"Come on over here, Lee. The movie is about to start." My mom says, patting the spot next to her left between her and my dad as Siah is sitting next to her right.

I grumble, holding onto my drink, and point to the empty spot beside uncle Aiden. "I want to sit beside uncle Aiden."

"You want to disturb your uncle when he needs all the rest he can get? Not a chance." My dad says and I whine, looking at Uncle Aiden with my face squeezed into a puppy look.

Uncle Aiden laughs at the look on my face. "Alright, come on, but only if you promise to stay still."

I light up instantly, nodding my head enthusiastically. "I promise!"

A laugh echoes from my mom. That makes me freeze. "Lee? Stay still? When has that ever happened?"

"I will stay still!" I whine and hurry to the spot next before he can go back on his word.

"You let her have her way a little too much, Aiden." My dad says, shaking his head.

Why are they always attacking him just because he's not like them?

"Oh, it's Kali, after all. Anything for my enchanting lucky charm"

My regular smile pops onto my face at the sound of hearing that. It always sounds so good to hear.

"The movie is starting!" Siah says, dragging everyone's attention away from us. While everyone focuses on the movie ahead, I can't help but glance up at Uncle Aiden and smile even more.

· ⋔ ·

"Mom!" I rush into the house, ignoring my dad's shout from outside instructing me not to run.

"Hey! Look who is back from school!" my mom says as she's coming out of the kitchen. She tries to hug me, but I'm in a hurry and I don't let her.

"Uncle Aiden is around, isn't he? I saw his car outside. He's here, isn't he?" I ask, excitement pooling in my voice.

My mom scoffs, shaking her head. "Of course, who else can make you this excited if not Aiden."

"Mommy!"

"Yes, yes! Fine! Your uncle Aiden is in Siah's room helping her with her assignment."

Siah's room?

I hurry away from my mom to my sister's room.

"Lee, why don't you get changed first!" she shouts, but I don't turn back to answer.

I open Siah's door without knocking, knowing how much it will piss her off.

"Urghh, Lee! How many times have I told you to knock before you open my room door?"

I ignore her and run to him. "Uncle Aiden!"

"Kali! How was school?"

"It was good! Why don't you come to my room? I'll tell you all about it!" I say, eager to get him away from Siah.

"Alright dear, let me be done with Siah's assignment first, okay?" he says with a light smile and then turns back to her desk.

"But..." I say, pulling up my go-to puppy eyes. "You've been helping her since!"

"Oh, stop being such a whining child. Go to your room and change out your uniform," Siah says and I glare at her but look back at Uncle Aiden with my lashes fluttering.

He chuckles only a bit and stretches his hand forwards to ruffle my hair. "Go on Kali. I'll meet you soon. We're almost done with her assignment, so I'll come by. So change, okay?" He says and turns away from me to Siah's assignment with his full attention.

I stare at him shocked. He's never pushed me aside before. Water pools in my eyes as I wait, wait for him to turn back around to face me, to stand up and tell me to lead the way, but he doesn't.

I turn away, but not before I see the grin on Siah's face, and I just know she's making fun of me. I tighten my fist as I storm out of the room, angry.

· ₪ ·

Have I done something wrong? Why is Uncle Aiden ignoring me again? He doesn't have time for me anymore and that's not fair. When dad mentioned Uncle Aiden got a new job that will need him to work from dad's study, I thought the fact that he'll be around all the time meant he'll stop postponing our time together.

But ever since he started this new job, he's not even looked at me, he's just been locked up in the study telling me he'll answer me some other time.

That some other time never comes.

But I will get his attention no matter what. I'll make him play with me again.

I open the door to dad's study and peep inside the large room filled with stacks of books that should be a crime in this world.

"Uncle Aiden?"

He looks up from the pile of papers on the desk he's arranging with a little smile. "Oh thank goodness, Kali. Can you bring those files from that table?" he asks, pointing to the table by the side which used to be Siah's table before I was born when she spent time with dad.

I go over to get the files with no restraint and walk over to him, putting on my best puppy smile.

He smiles and collects the files from me, offering me a brief thank you, but otherwise spares me no other glance.

"Uncle Aiden?" My voice comes out so mushy I almost think it's not mine as it's so different from how I feel inside. "Aren't you going to play with me?"

"Not now, Kali, some other time, okay?" His gaze doesn't even flicker to me but remains on the files as he continues to sort them out.

"But that's what you've been saying all this time!" I whine and stamp my foot for even more effect.

He never liked it when I whined before. He once told me if I wanted anything from him, all I had to do was whine and his attention would be all mine because he didn't like it when his enchanting lucky charm whined.

"Kali," He groans, turning to face me with a disapproving gaze, and then he turns away.

"Uncle Aiden," I whimper, pulling at his cloth so he will at least look at me.

Uncle Aiden turns abruptly, removing my hand from his cloth, making me stumble and fall on my butt.

I freeze up, wide-eyed, staring at him.

Did he, just, push me?

"Oh my goodness, Kali, I'm so sorry!" he exclains, lowering himself to my height on the floor.

I scramble away from him with bulging eyes, my body trembling. Right in front of me, his face contorts. Something is changing.

He hesitates, looking at me with a cautioned gaze, searching my face. "Kali?"

I am not sure what he sees on my face, all I know is that in that split second, the edge of my lips curl up and my eyes harden.

It happens in just one split second but the moment it's gone and Uncle Aiden tries to come closer after his hesitation, everything had changed.

What just happened has changed. The image in front of me has twirled and spun and all I see is hurt.

"Kali?"

I bolt up from my position shaking and rushing out of the room, tears from nowhere spilling from my eyes. Not long after, I stumble into my mom, whose attention zeroes in on my injured arm. She stops me instantly and tugs on my arm, looking at the slight injury there.

"Lee? How did you get injured?"

She turns me to face her, and that's when she sees the tears in my eyes and looks in the direction I'm coming from.

"What happened?"

The story that spills from my lips seems foreign, but I can't stop it from coming out. It suddenly feels like I have no control over my body. Terrors build up in my eyes as my sobs increase. "It's him, Uncle Aiden. H- he- he hurt me."

My mom's body goes rigid with the hug and looks up towards my back where my dad is standing.

Everything else from that point becomes a blur.

Uncle Aiden hurt me in a way no uncle should. My uncle Aiden, who only calls me Kali, became my worst nightmare.

These statements weave themselves into my mind, forming a complete story on its own like a twisted cloth draped over my body and stuck, not wanting to come off.

"How could he? How dare he touch my little girl? I thought..."

My mom and I sob into ourselves as she convinces me it's fine, he would never hurt me again.

Sirens fill the house the next minute, along with shouts from two adult voices.

"You'll rot in jail for laying your hands on my daughter, Aiden! Is that what this was about? Staying in my house?" My dad shouts as the police drag him off.

"What are you saying, Keith?! That's not true. Kali!" He shouts once they reach the living room and I wince.

My mom pushes me behind her to shield me from him. "Don't talk to her!"

He struggles against the police as he tries to get me to look at him.

"Kali, please tell your parents the truth! I didn't touch you. I would never do that to you. Kalisha! You said you like me. Don't destroy my life like this!"

"Take him away!" My daddy growls, but I turn to look at him as I continue weeping in my mom's hands.

"Kali!" He growls. "Don't do this. You'll regret this. Kali, you will pay for this! You'll pay for ruining my life!"

It's the last thing he says before he's dragged off and the door shuts out any of his other shouts.

But shouldn't he be the one to pay for hurting me? I'm not ruining his life, he's just getting what he deserves.

□ · □□□□□□ · ℕ · □□□□□□ · □

✎Word Count: 2,046

✎Total Word Count: 18,817

Vote, Comment, and Share if you enjoyed it!

□ · □□□□□□ · ℕ · □□□□□□ · □

☐ · ☐☐☐☐☐ · ₪ · ☐☐☐☐☐ · ☐

☐ LIGHT FLOODS THE DARKNESS as I gasp, opening my eyes. Whirring sound crashes into the relative peace I remember being conscious too.

Sharp pangs drill through every inch of my body that I can't pinpoint exactly where it's coming from.

I try to make sense of where I am, but a wide-eyed figure covers the light, causing my heart to skip for a tad bit at the sudden movement.

I'm thrown right back to everything that happened and so when I'm engulfed in a hug, I push against the person with no regard for the searing pain it causes me.

"I'm so sorry. I..."

"It's Haveal. It was him all along. He..."

"Yes, I know! They know! It's fine! They know. He's been arrested, okay? He's gone to where he belongs. So you're fine now, okay? You're alright."

The airy voice that is always so calm but is shaky instead steadily reaches my ears. It takes a minute for me to recognize her voice and when I do, my beating heart slows down its pace and my rigid body relaxes. "Rea?" I croak.

Reagan moves carefully this time and engulfs me in a hug, sobbing into my shoulder. "Yes, it's me." She sobs. "It's me and you're okay. Oh my goodness, I was so scared! You're okay." She repeats twice before she draws back, holding both of my cheeks to look into my face.

Something dulled her ever bright set of Sienna Brown eyes, filling it with a squinted gaze as she stares into mine.

I'm not sure what she finds there, but she says nothing and instead pulls me into a hug again.

"I'm sorry, ma'am, but you can't handle the patient like that." A fierce voice calls out from before us, making us spring apart.

I turn to the woman wearing a medic attire and that makes me finally focus away on my surroundings.

The patient?

I look down at my body to see different patches of bandages all over. Looking up, I realize I woke up to be nothing but the in-car light of an ambulance.

The dark sky is in full control outside the ambulance, lightened up by the red and blue light of the police cars surrounding Shaveal robotics.

"Of course. I'm so sorry, I was just..."

Reagan's voice pulls me back before my thoughts can run wild.

The medic lady, squinting her eyes at Reagan, waves her off in understanding before focusing back on me.

"How do you feel now, Ma'am?" The lady asks.

How do I feel? How do I describe how I feel right now?

With the raised eyebrow of both the woman and Rea, I take in deep breaths and force out an answer that sums it up. "I don't know."

The medic looks down at my body as I do.

"You passed out because you were losing a lot of blood. Some of which were coming from slashes already getting infected. You'd need to take it all easy right now," she explains, her fierce tone dripped with care.

"Right," I say, not sure what exactly I should say. There's just so much going on that I don't understand. "How..." I start, but I can't finish my sentence.

My breaths go in shallow as I'm swamped with images of everything that happened. I can't...

Warmth fills my hands, pulling me back out. I turn to my side to see a soft smile on Reagan's lips with her hands holding mine, the source of the warmth. 'You're alright now,' she mouths.

I take a deep breath, nodding. I take another try. "How did they know?"

"An alarm," Reagan chirps in. "They said someone pressed the emergency alarm."

"Do you think you're good enough to give the police your statement before we leave?" The lady asks.

My statement? They want me to relive it all by telling them when everything still seems like a harsh joke to me?

My eyes flicker to the building by the side of the opened door. It all feels like a dream, except the pain I feel at any movement I make is a reality check.

"I think we'll wait a bit," Reagan replies with her eyes locked on me. "She'll need to get a grasp on things before she can fully give them the right statement they need. I'm sure they can understand that."

It's times like this, I'm glad to have a therapist as a friend. Reading into situations has always been her best feat, and it helped in situations like this when I can't even put my thoughts together.

I nod in agreement when the lady looks at me for confirmation. She hesitates, watching me as if I'd change my mind in that second before she turns away howling out some instructions to some other people.

"Hey," Reagan calls out to me, but before she can say anything else, loud murmuring voices cut in close to the opened door. Instead of just passing by, the murmuring stops right in front of the opened door as the group notices me sitting up. The group of four spread out in front of me, watching me with wide, cautioned eyes. They all look like siblings with similarities in their expressions.

"Kalisha! Oh thank goodness, you're awake!" Charlotte's honeyed tone rings out louder than it normally would, but with sincerity, it has never had with me.

I squint at them with just one question clawing itself in my mind. Where on earth were they? When our boss was busy finding pleasure in torturing my life?

Reagan's calm posture stiffens at their presence by my side. She shifts even closer, and I recognize it as her protective stance.

I know she's thinking the same question I am. This little action makes me want to smile, but I don't.

"Oh my goodness, I'm so sorry you had to go through that," Emily voices out, her voice dripping with empathy and there's a remnant of tears in her eyes.

Go through what? I want to ask. What exactly does everyone know about what happened?

"I never would have thought Haveal would have been capable of hurting anyone."

Neither did I.

Even though I know having anyone go through the torment I went through with me would not help the sinking feeling I feel, the question that has popped into my mind since they stopped in front of me pours out of my lips. "Where were you guys when it was going on?" The accusing tone is not at all hidden in my croaked voice.

"Don't give us that tone." Theodore cut in, recognizing the accusation instantly. He squints his eyes at me. "Haveal made us move after telling us the venue had changed. We couldn't have known what was going on."

Darren nudges him with his elbow and a little shake of his head.

Charlotte takes in the opportunity. "We definitely thought it was creepy," she says, drawing my attention to her, her voice drips with sour sweetness.

I squint at her, but it does nothing to stop her flow of speech.

"But I mean it was Haveal. There's really no one who can confront him, well maybe except you, but you were running late so we all just moved to the ground floor..."

Her words flow into the background of my thoughts with my thoughts refocusing on Haveal. He had cleared the way so perfectly, but there's just one thing that's still a bother for me.

Sure, he gave the whole garbage about hating me because of my name, but something doesn't add up.

Why had Haveal chosen this day suddenly to destroy my life?

"... Enchanting lucky charm..."

I freeze up and grab Charlotte's wavering hand, choking the rest of her words into her mouth.

Everyone's attention snaps to me at my sudden reaction. Charlotte stares at me with wide, frightened eyes, wondering what's going on.

"What did you say?!"

She grumbles, struggling against my firm grip when I don't release her hand at her gaze.

"What did you just say?!"

"Let go of me first you bitch!" she screams, instantly pulling her hand from mine and throwing me her regular piercing glare, but my hard gaze doesn't die.

Reagan moves even closer, ready to stop any fight that can take place whilst putting all her attention on me. Her eyes flicker around my face, trying to decipher what's up, but this is no time for a Q and A session.

"It's just what the client told him while he was telling us about the change of venue," Darren says.

"And what did he say?" I grit out, holding my breath. There's no way I heard right. I'm in over my head because of that memory.

"Why are you so hung up on it?! It doesn't matter what the client said?" Charlotte retorts, furrowing her brows at me.

"Just answer the damn question!"

"Calm your horses, geez!" She rolls her eyes at me then sighs, "He said and I quote: 'Anything for my enchanting lucky charm.'"

I wheeze, frozen in place. There's a cracking noise on repeat in my head, matching the startled noise out of it. Everything crashes into each other, and I can't make sense of anything.

"Please... needs... space." Rea's words break in and out of my head, followed by the murmuring of my colleagues, but it's no business of mine as the air suddenly feels limited.

He can't possibly be here. No! There's no way that can happen. I made sure...

I- I did that. I made sure he was to spend the rest of his life in prison, never to set foot in the real world again. Never to...

Sound familiar?

You'll pay for this, Kali! You'll pay for ruining my life.

You designed this situation, forged the story and started this game. It was you, mother.

I sputter, choking on nothing but my thoughts.

I'm yanked into a hug with soft pats going up and down my back, but it has absolutely no soothing effect on me.

"You're fine now, Lee! You're safe and everything's fine. Nothing can happen to you again."

But that's far from the truth, Reagan. Everything can happen to me now because nothing is fine. No, it's far from it. I ruined someone's life and now he is back to ruin mine.

I stare into the darkness ahead, and the edges of my lips curl up. Since the truth behind the lie I have lived for 22 years is creeping up to the light, then there's no need to hide anymore.

The darkness within my soul has been ignited like an embered coal ready to consume everything within its path.

I've been asleep for too long.

□ · □□□□□□ · ₪ · □□□□□□ · □

THE END.

Lightning Source UK Ltd.
Milton Keynes UK
UKHW010646030123
414755UK00014B/464